This Little Hippo
book belongs to

_____

_____

For Olivia –
NM

For Emma –
KL

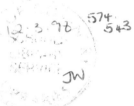

Scholastic Children's Books,
Commonwealth House, 1-19 New Oxford Street,
London WC1A 1NU, UK
a division of Scholastic Ltd

London ~ New York ~ Toronto ~ Sydney ~ Auckland
Mexico City ~ New Delhi ~ Hong Kong

First published by Scholastic Ltd, 1997

Text copyright © Nicola Moon, 1997
Illustrations copyright © Karin Littlewood, 1997

ISBN 0 590 19578 6

Printed in Spain

Billy's Sunflower

by Nicola Moon
Illustrated by Karin Littlewood

Little Hippo

Billy had a beautiful sunflower that he'd grown from a seed.

It was taller than Billy.

It was taller than his big sister Laura.

It was taller than his Mum.

It was even taller than his Dad.

Every day Billy looked at its bright
green leaves. Every day he admired
its golden yellow petals. Every day
he looked up at its tall straight stem.

"My flower is as tall as the sky,"
he told his friends.

One day Billy noticed something
different about his flower.

The bright green leaves didn't seem so bright. The golden yellow petals weren't quite so golden. And the tall straight stem wasn't quite so straight.

"What's wrong with my flower?"
he asked Dad.
"Perhaps it needs water," said Dad,
as he rushed off to work.

So Billy watered his flower.

But the next day it was worse.

The bright green leaves were
wrinkled and droopy. The golden
yellow petals were turning brown.
And the tall straight stem had bent
over at the top.

Billy looked up at his sad,
brown sunflower.

"What's wrong with my flower?" he
  asked Laura.
"It's autumn," said Laura, and ran off
  to play with her friends.

"What is autumn?" Billy asked the girls.
"It's when leaves turn brown," said Sally.
"And days become shorter," said Clare.
"And flowers die," said Laura.

Billy ran indoors to Mum.

"My flower's got autumn and it's getting shorter and turning brown and Laura says it's going to die!" he cried.

Mum dried his tears.

"Autumn is when the world gets ready for winter," she explained. "The winter would be too cold and dark for your flower."
Billy felt really sad.
"I don't think I like autumn," he said.

He went out to look at his flower.
It looked even more withered and brown,
and the old sad flower was drooping down.
"I don't want you to die," said Billy.
A gust of wind rustled in the dying leaves,
as if the flower was trying to speak.

Then Billy felt something.

PLOP!

Something landed on his head.

PLOP!

There it was again.

PLOP! PLOP!

And again and again.

"My flower is raining!" cried Billy.
"My flower is raining SEEDS!"
He ran indoors to find
Mum and Dad and Laura.

They gathered up a big bag of seeds.
"We can put them on the bird table,
 when winter comes," said Mum.
"The birds will be hungry in the cold weather."

"Not all the seeds,' said Billy,
   picking out five of the biggest shiniest
   seeds. "I'm going to keep these ones."

When the winter came, Billy watched the birds flocking to the bird table to eat the seeds from his flower.

And when the winter had gone
at last, he took his five special
seeds and planted them carefully
in the garden.

"I'm going to grow the tallest
sunflowers in the world!" said Billy.
"Taller than Dad?" asked Laura.
"Taller than anyone," said Billy.